First Dog

By
Patricia Quinn Hays

Introduction by
Bishop John M. Quinn

Illustrations by
Julie Victor

saint mary's press

The publishing team included Jerry Ruff, development editor; Brian Holzworth, designer; and John Vitek, publisher. Prepress and manufacturing coordinated by the production departments of Saint Mary's Press.

Cover image © Julie Victor

Printed in the United States of America

4349 (PO3897)

ISBN 978-1-59982-273-0, hardcover

Library of Congress Cataloging-in-Publication Data

Hays, Patricia Quinn.
  First dog / by Patricia Quinn Hays ; introduction by Bishop John M. Quinn ; illustrations by Julie Victor.
      p. cm.
  ISBN 978-1-59982-273-0 (hardcover)—ISBN 978-1-59982-274-7 (softcover)—ISBN 978-1-59982-275-4 (ebook) 1. Dogs—Fiction. 2. Christmas stories. I. Title.
  PS3608.A9855F57 2012
  813'.6—dc23
                                                                                      2012028083

Introduction

What a special joy for me to introduce my sister's book, *First Dog*, which is a Christmas story about wanting to belong and hoping to have a family.

The Feast of Christmas is about the Incarnation, an event of love in which the Father sends his only Son, born of a Virgin, whose name is Mary. Christmas is about the overflowing love of God and how that love opens our hearts to others.

There are many stories and legends that retell the message of the overflowing love of God for us in the Incarnation. All of us have a favorite. Perhaps you remember the story of *Amahl and the Night Visitors*, about a lame little boy who meets up with the Magi and is healed when he comes to the manger. I treasure *A Christmas Carol*, in which Scrooge is changed into a loving man after he awakens on Christmas morning from dreams that show him his past. Another favorite is the legend of the *Little Drummer Boy*, who had nothing to bring to the Baby Jesus as a gift, so he played his drum and the Child Jesus smiled at him. Now you will read another story about Christmas, and I hope it helps you to live a faith-filled and generous life all year long.

This book honors our parents, George and Mary Quinn, and all the proceeds will go to the Catholic schools in the Diocese of Winona, Minnesota.

Most Reverend John M. Quinn
Bishop of Winona, Minnesota
May 2012

A very long time ago in a far-away city called Nazareth, there lived a carpenter, Joseph, and his wife, Mary. While they were eagerly awaiting the birth of Mary's baby, Joseph received some difficult news.

"Mary," said Joseph. "We must travel to Bethlehem. It will be a long journey."

A decree had come from Caesar Augustus that all persons must be counted for the census. Since Joseph's family came from Bethlehem, he and Mary had to travel there to be enrolled. Joseph and Mary set out for Bethlehem. Joseph walked and Mary rode a donkey. They knew that the baby could be born at any time and the journey to Bethlehem was very long.

When they arrived in Bethlehem it was getting late, and Joseph and Mary were tired and needed a place to rest. Bethlehem was crowded with many other travelers, already in town for the census! Joseph and Mary stopped at several inns to seek shelter, but there was no room for them. Each innkeeper said, "Sorry, no rooms for rent." Or, "This inn is completely filled." Or, "Oh no, you can't stay here."

It also happened that at the same time a scruffy, little dog was wandering near one of the inns, hoping to find some food to eat and a family to care for him. Just yesterday, the dog's owner had sent him into the streets, saying: "I can't afford to keep you any longer. I can barely feed my own children, let alone a hungry animal."

So, out into the streets of Bethlehem the little dog bravely wandered. When he came to the doorway of an inn or a home hoping to find some food, people yelled, "Go away!" Other people chased the dog with a broom and shouted, "Shoo!" Some groups of children playing in the streets threw stones and sticks at the frightened little dog.

"What a sad way to live," the little dog thought. "I have no place to call home and I must beg for food every day."

The little dog scampered down the streets of Bethlehem, hoping a friendly person would give him some table scraps. He had no place to stay and no food. And now he was cold too.

Then, the most amazing thing happened. In the moonlight, the little dog saw the outline of a stable at the end of the street near the inns. He came closer to the stable and saw the door was open—so he looked inside.

To his surprise, two small lambs, a cow, and a donkey were nestled together in the straw. "Welcome, come in," the animals said to the dog. "We have never met you before. Did you just come to Bethlehem with all of the travelers?"

"No," replied the dog. "I had a family here in Bethlehem that cared for me. I had a home and food, but they couldn't afford to keep me. Now I have no family, no food to eat, and no place to stay."

"Why don't you stay with us?" the animals said. "There is plenty of room here in the stable and the straw will keep you warm. There is water in the corner if you are thirsty and some hay for you to eat. It's all we have, but we will share it with you."

The little dog lapped up the water, but could not eat the hay. "I'll rest a while," he said, "but I must go back into the streets and see if a traveler or an innkeeper will give me something to eat."

"By the way," asked the lamb, "what is your name?"

"I don't have a name," said the little dog. "My family never gave me a name. They already had several children, two other dogs, and three cats. I think they knew they couldn't keep me and if they gave me a name, it would be harder for them to let me go. I really miss them and the children."

It was now evening, and the little dog awoke after sleeping for about a half hour. He said to the other animals: "I'll be back soon. I need to go into the streets and see if I can find some food."

Carefully, the little dog walked to the street where the inns were and waited for a traveler, hoping for at least a scrap of food. Then the dog saw Joseph and Mary. He heard Joseph say to Mary: "It looks like no one will take us in tonight. There is not even a small room for us. Mary, I don't know what to do and the baby will be here soon."

The little dog thought to himself: "They need a place to rest, just like I do. They can stay in the stable with the lambs, the cow, the donkey, and me. It's just down the street, but how do I get them to follow me?"

The little dog walked up to Joseph and Mary. He barked and ran toward the stable. At first, they did not understand. They started to go the other way. So the little dog barked louder and louder and started running back and forth in the direction of the stable.

"Joseph," said Mary, "I think this little dog is trying to lead us somewhere. He wants us to follow him. I must rest before the baby comes. We have nowhere else to go. Let's follow the dog and see where he is leading us."

The little dog led them to the stable with the lambs, the cow, and the donkey. Joseph said to Mary, "It's a barn! Do you want to stay here?" Mary looked at Joseph and said, "It will be all right." Joseph then patted the little dog on the head, and to thank him he opened his traveling bag and gave him some bread to eat. The little dog wagged his tail because he felt loved and appreciated. He then curled up in the straw, and in just a few minutes, he went to sleep.

Later that very night, the little dog awoke to the sound of a baby crying. He opened his eyes and saw that Mary had given birth to a beautiful baby boy and had laid him in the manger. The little dog, along with the other animals, huddled together with Mary, Joseph, and the tiny baby. Together they kept each other warm.

Baby Jesus, the King of Kings, had been born!

It was the first Christmas.

Not long after the birth of the baby, the little dog heard the sounds of people coming down the street toward the stable. He barked and barked and stood by the door of the stable until Joseph told him that it was okay to let these strangers inside. They were shepherds who had come from the fields outside the village. An angel had told them to go and find the newborn Savior wrapped in swaddling clothes, lying in a manger.

Later, the little dog heard other people coming down the street. He looked out the door and saw three Wise Men riding on top of animals he had never seen before. He barked and barked and nipped at their hooves. Joseph said to the little dog: "It's okay! There's no need to bark— those are camels! We need to welcome these strangers inside too." These Wise Men explained to Mary and Joseph how they had seen a bright star that appeared in the Eastern sky. They knew it was the sign that a King had been born. They followed the star until they came to the place where Jesus lay. They had brought Him gifts of gold, frankincense, and myrrh.

That night, a wonderful thing happened. In this desert land, it began to snow! The softly falling snow covered everything in glistening white.

With all the visitors coming to the stable, the little dog made certain that his place was close to the manger to protect the baby. He hoped he had found his new family.

Joseph said to Mary: "Tomorrow we will be leaving. What shall we do about the dog? No one has come looking for him and I don't think that he has any place to go. Remember that he found shelter for us when no one else would take us in."

When the dog heard Mary and Joseph talking about him, he snuggled even closer to the Baby Jesus and his little tail wagged. Just then, the Baby Jesus opened his eyes, looked at the dog, and smiled.

Joseph was a carpenter and he made wooden chairs and tables to sell. He said to Mary: "I could use a dog around my carpentry shop. He could be our watch dog. And as Jesus grows older, the dog could play with Him and be His friend."

The little dog perked up his ears, but he was afraid to pick up his head or open his eyes. "Maybe . . . just maybe, I have found my family," he thought to himself.

Mary said: "If we are going to keep him as part of our family, we will have to give him a name. What will we call the dog?"

Joseph looked at the dog and thought for a few moments. "His name will be Lucky. He will be our protector." When the dog heard his new name, he looked up and let out a soft bark! "Listen to him," said Joseph. "He likes his new name."

What a happy dog Lucky was! He had found his new family, and he finally had a name. Most of all, he had a little boy to grow with, to play with, and to protect. He was the happiest dog in the whole world.

Lucky thought to himself, "I am the luckiest dog in the whole world, because I belong to Jesus, the King of Kings."

Lucky's most important jobs were to protect, care for, and play with Jesus every day. Lucky held the "first place" among all the dogs in the world, because he would grow up with Jesus Christ, the eternal Son of God, born of the Virgin Mary.

"We will leave in the morning," said Joseph.

Lucky knew he was part of the Holy Family, and that this was just the beginning of many great adventures!

Patricia Quinn Hays is the second of three children of the late George and Mary Quinn. Her elder brother, George, is now deceased. Patricia and her younger brother, John, grew up on the east side of Detroit, where they attended Our Lady of Good Counsel Elementary School, followed by Dominican High School for Patricia and St. Anthony High School for John.

Patricia currently lives in Grosse Pointe Farms, Michigan. After 50 years of marriage, her husband, Robert, passed away in September 2011. They have three children and two grandsons. The children are Barbara, Susan (Vince) Marrs, and Jeffrey. Andrew and Alexander Marrs are their grandsons.

Bishop John Michael Quinn

is the youngest of the three children of the late George and Mary Quinn. He was ordained a Catholic priest on March 17, 1972.

He served as director of the education department of the Archdiocese of Detroit from 1990 until his ordination as an auxiliary bishop for Detroit in 2003.

In October 2008 he was appointed Coadjutor Bishop of Winona, Minnesota, by His Holiness, Pope Benedict XVI. In May 2009 he became the eighth Bishop of Winona, where he currently serves.

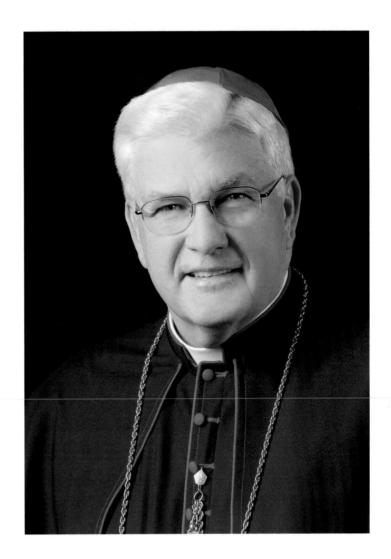

Lucky is based on our family dog, Beauregard, also called Bobo, who came on Christmas 1971 as a gift from our brother George to our mom. This was our first Christmas after Dad's death in November 1971.

Bobo was Mom's faithful companion and protector, until Mom entered eternal life on October 11, 1984.

This book is dedicated to the memory of our
parents, George P. and Mary D. Quinn, who
gave us Christmas every day.

Acknowledgments

Our deepest appreciation to Fr. Timothy R. Pelc, pastor of St. Ambrose Church in Grosse Pointe Park, Michigan, for his valuable assistance with the text and layout of the book.